SUPER
HEROES

BATMAN™

TALES OF THE
BATCAVE

THE FROZEN ZONE
FREEZE RAY

by
MICHAEL DAHL

illustrated by
LUCIANO VECCHIO

Batman created by
BOB KANE WITH BILL FINGER

STONE ARCH BOOKS
a capstone imprint

Published by Stone Arch Books in 2018
A Capstone Imprint
1710 Roe Crest Drive
North Mankato, Minnesota 56003
www.mycapstone.com

STAR39737

Library of Congress Cataloging-in-Publication Data is available on the Library of
Congress website.

ISBN: 978-1-4965-5977-7 (library binding)
ISBN: 978-1-4965-5985-2 (paperback)
ISBN: 978-1-4965-5997-5 (eBook PDF)

Summary: A jewelry store robbery sets Batman and Robin hot on the trail of Mr. Freeze
and his new cold-zone freeze ray weapon.

Editor: Christopher Harbo
Designer: Brann Garvey

Printed and bound in the USA.
010831S18

TABLE OF CONTENTS

This is the BATCAVE.

DANGEROUS
FREEZE RAY

It is the secret headquarters of Batman and his crime-fighting partner, Robin.

Hundreds of trophies, awards, and souvenirs fill the Batcave's hidden rooms. Each one tells a story of danger, villainy, and victory.

This is the tale of a dangerous freeze ray that is now displayed in the Batcave . . .

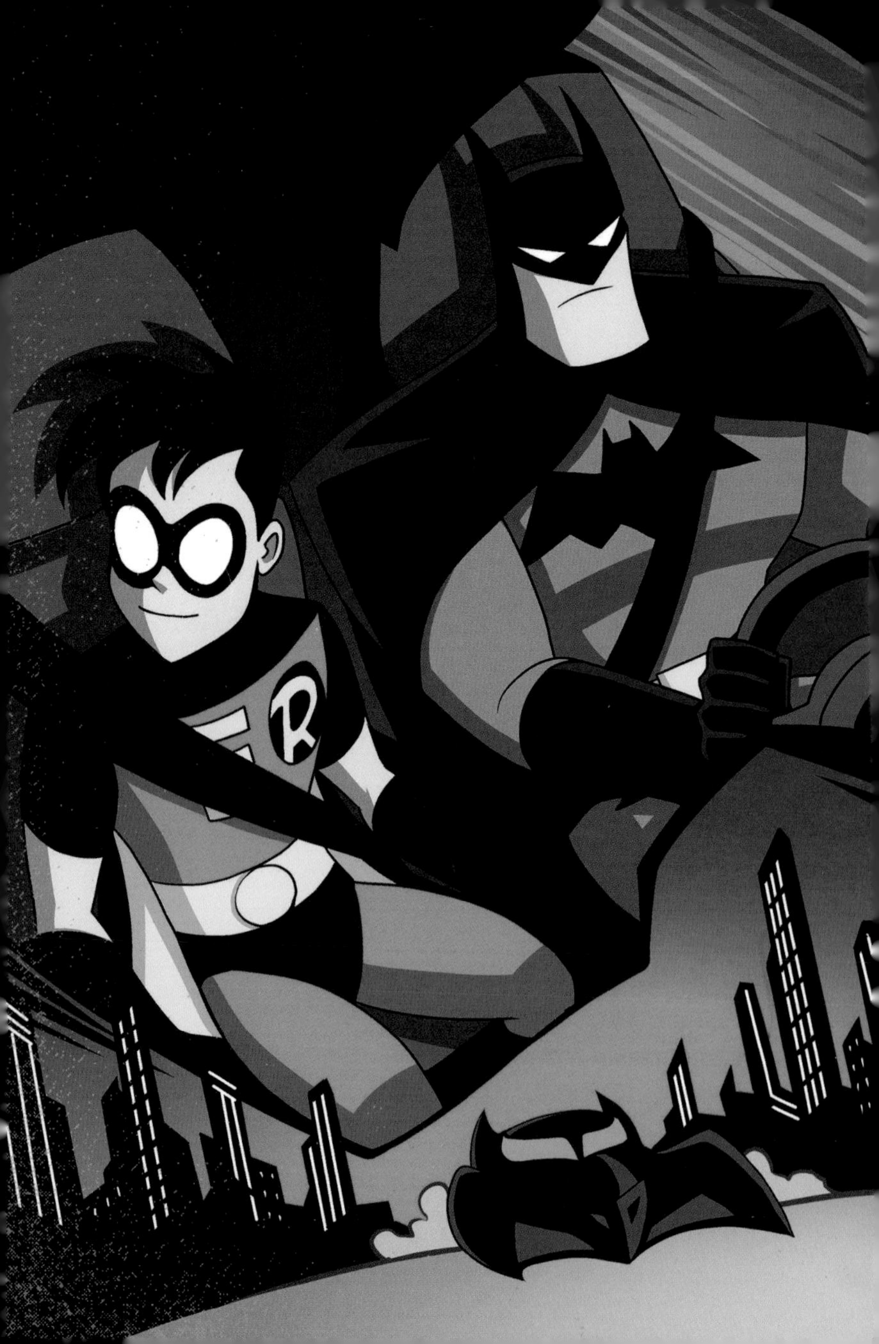

CHAPTER 1

TOO COOL

"Pull over, Batman!" cries Robin. "Something really weird is going on!"

Batman and Robin are patrolling Gotham City in the Batmobile.

The Caped Crusader pulls to the curb.

People on the sidewalk are shivering.

The Dynamic Duo leap from the car.

"H-h-help us!" cries a woman. "I c-c-can't st-st-st-stop sh-sh-shivering!"

"What's wrong, ma'am? Are you frightened?" Robin asks.

"They're not shaking with fear, Robin," says Batman. "They're shivering from the cold."

"The cold looks likes it's spreading!" says Robin. He points to a nearby store. Its window is covered in frost on a warm summer day.

The window belongs to Dudley's Diamonds.

"This is not cool," says Robin.

The two heroes race inside the store.

Thieves dressed in snowsuits are breaking glass counters. They yank jewels from their cases. They shove them into big canvas bags.

In the middle of the room stands a tall figure. His strange uniform is topped by a clear glass helmet.

He carries a deadly looking weapon. The weapon is aimed right at the two heroes.

"Mr. Freeze," says the Dark Knight.

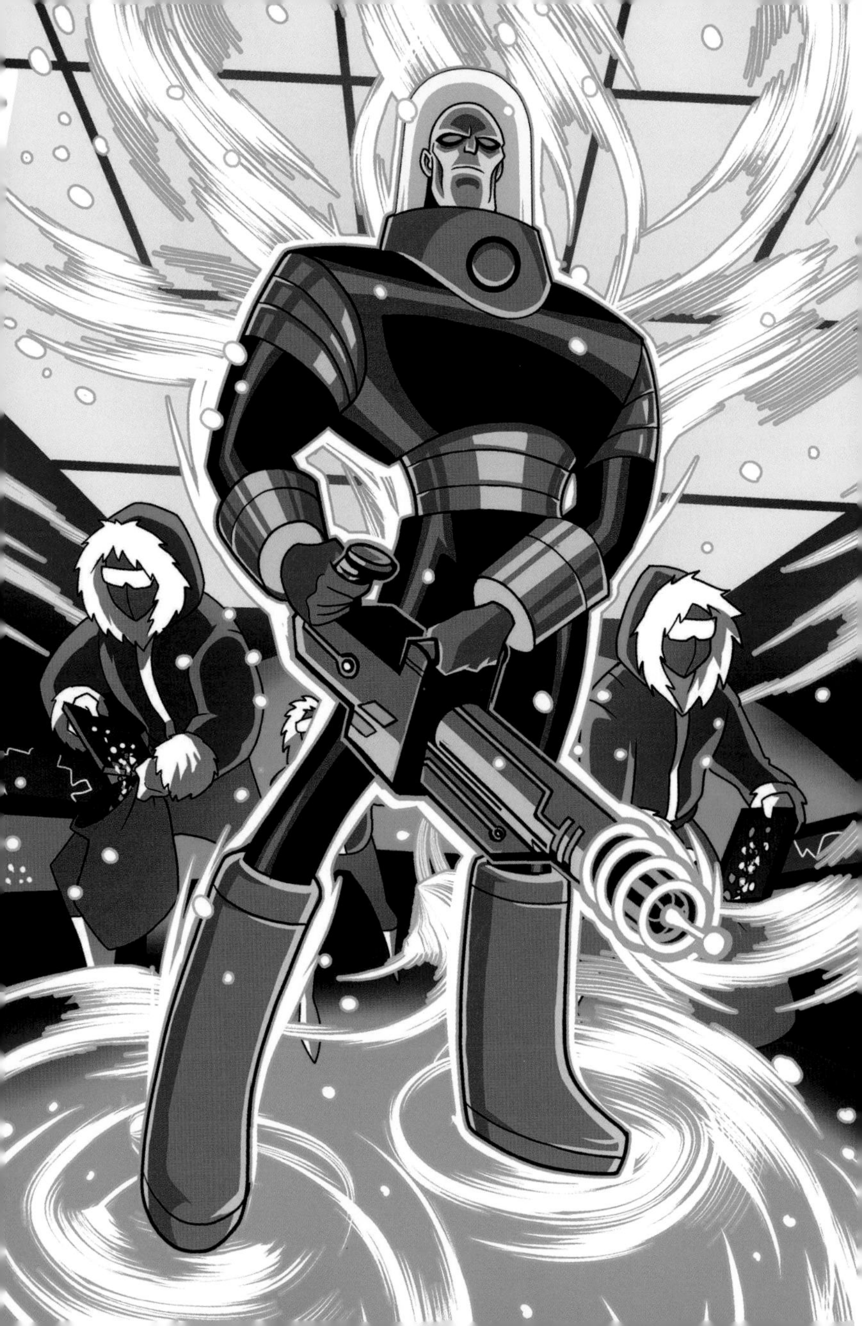

CHAPTER 2

COLD ZONE

"Beware my new weapon," warns Mr. Freeze.

The villain nods toward the freeze ray in his hands. "My freeze ray creates a Zone of Cold. Anyone who gets near me will feel its icy grip!"

Snow covers the store's floor. Icicles hang from the ceiling.

"He's not kidding," says Robin.

"Then why aren't you two shivering?" says Mr. Freeze angrily.

"Our uniforms protect us from heat and cold," says Batman.

"No matter," says Mr. Freeze. "My weapon works the old way too."

Suddenly, dozens of icicles blast out of the freeze ray.

The icy spears pin Robin's cape to the wall. A frosty gag forms over his mouth.

Robin can't speak or shout a warning to Batman. But the Caped Crusader flips through the air to avoid a second ice attack.

The villain triggers his weapon and creates an ice-slide tunnel.

"Stay cool, Batman," Mr. Freeze yells. "I'm sure we'll meet again!"

Then the villain jumps into the chute along with his men. They quickly slip away.

Batman peels the icy gag off Robin. The Boy Wonder drops to his knees. He is weak from the attack.

Robin looks up at Batman. Through blue lips he says, "I'm s-s-so cold! Y-Y-You have to stop him, B-B-Batman."

"Easier said than done, Boy Wonder," Batman replies. "I'm afraid Mr. Freeze is just warming up."

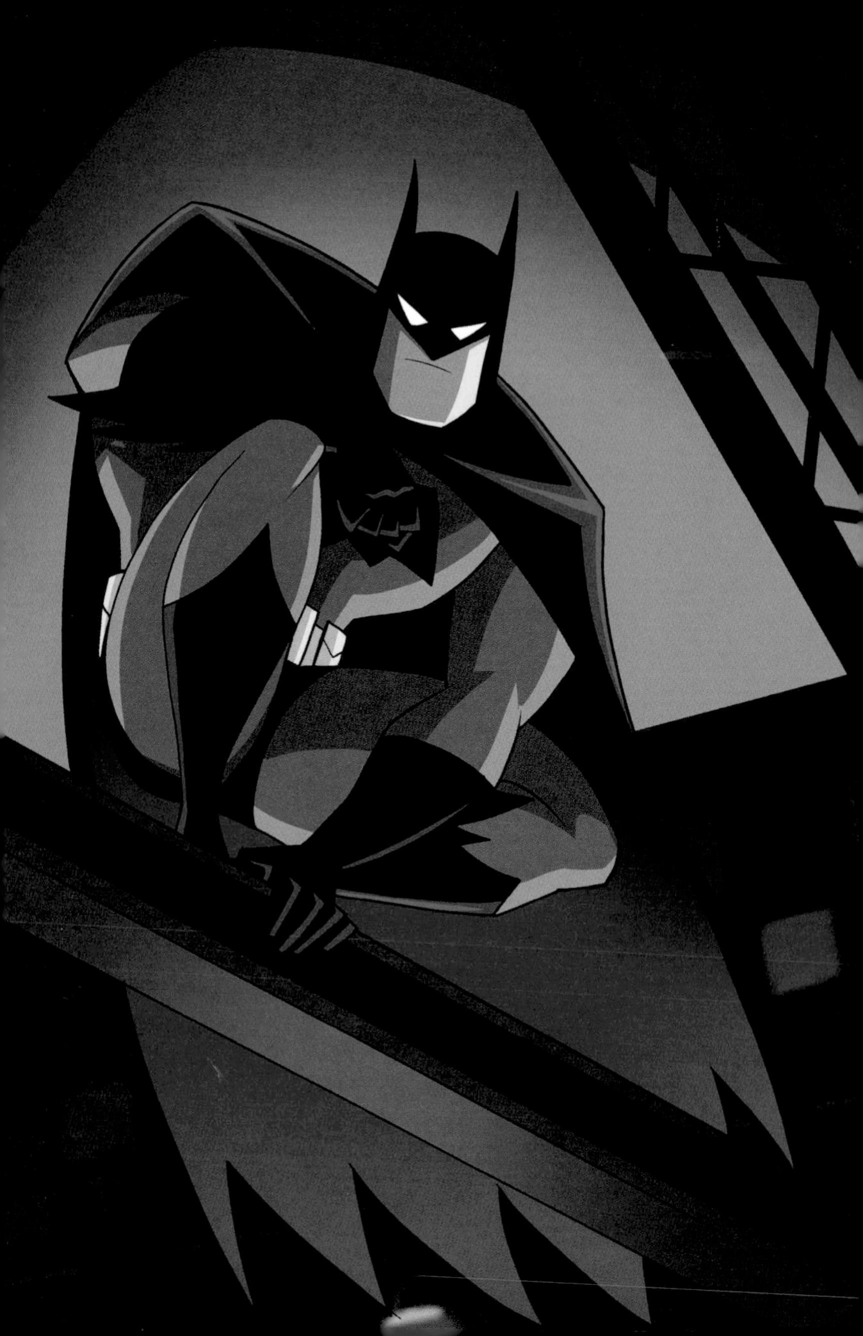

CHAPTER 3

SECRET ICE

A short while later, night falls on Gotham Harbor. Batman lurks in the shadows inside a large warehouse.

A special delivery is on its way to the warehouse. A secret crate of diamonds has been sent by ship from Spain.

Batman knows that criminals often call diamonds "ice."

If this expensive ice doesn't bring Mr. Freeze in from the cold, Batman thinks, *then nothing will.*

Batman can feel cool air flowing into the warehouse from vents overhead. The cool air is perfect for cargo that needs to stay cold.

Mr. Freeze should feel right at home here, thinks the Dark Knight.

CREEEE-EEE-EAKK!

A metal door at the far end of the warehouse begins to rise. A forklift rolls through the open door with a large crate on its two front arms.

Batman knows the crate holds the priceless diamonds. They're on a necklace called the Stars of Barcelona.

CRUNCH!

A tube of ice breaks through a wall.

Mr. Freeze has arrived in his getaway tunnel.

CHAPTER 4

FEEL THE FREEZE

An icy blast hits the forklift.

The forklift driver stops. He can't drive because he is shaking so much.

Batman steps forward. "Give it up, Mr. Freeze," he says.

Mr. Freeze is surprised. He stares at his foe. "Hmm, it's time to give my frost a bit more bite!" he says.

Mr. Freeze turns a dial on his weapon. The Zone of Cold grows stronger and wider.

Frost crawls across the floor toward Batman. The deep chill reaches through the hero's uniform.

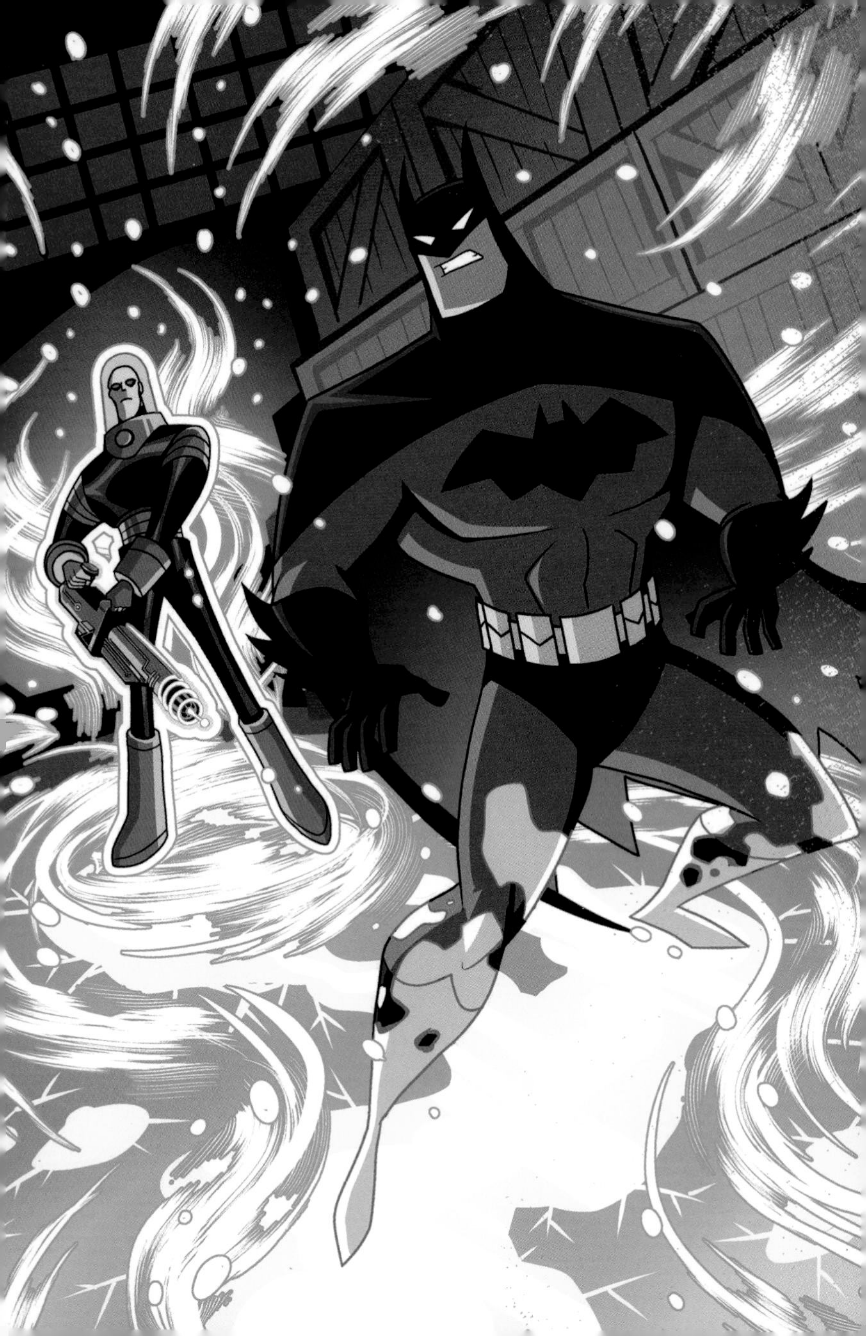

"You look lonely, Batman," says Mr. Freeze. "I heard your partner came down with a bad cold. Ha ha ha!"

Mr. Freeze steps toward the large crate.

Batman shouts, "Is this what you're looking for, Mr. Freeze?"

The Caped Crusader reaches into his Utility Belt. He pulls out a dazzling necklace.

"The Stars of Barcelona!" Mr. Freeze gasps.

CHAPTER 5

ZONING OUT

"Bring me the ice!" commands Mr. Freeze.

"The jewels belong to the people of Gotham City," Batman says.

"If you won't move," says Mr. Freeze, "then I'll make sure you never move again!"

The villain turns a dial on his weapon.

"You'll be the first victim of my maximum power!" he snarls. "I've never turned the Zone of Cold this high before!"

The freeze ray begins to shiver. It shakes and shudders in Mr. Freeze's hands.

Snow swirls through the warehouse. Thick frost crawls up the villain's arms and covers his helmet.

"I can't see!" Mr. Freeze shouts.

Mr. Freeze shoots his freeze ray. "I'll still get you, Batman!" he cries.

Suddenly, the forklift drives between Batman and the deadly weapon.

"Jump on!" cries the forklift driver.

As Batman leaps onto the vehicle, Robin throws off his forklift driver disguise. The Boy Wonder drives them to safety.

Mr. Freeze keeps shooting his freeze ray as he turns in a circle.

Unable to see, the villain creates a wall of ice around him. He is trapped.

"Watch this!" says Robin.

The Boy Wonder turns the forklift around. He drives it into the ice wall.

SMAAASHHHHHH!

The wall shatters. Chunks of ice crash down around Mr. Freeze. His weapon powers down beneath an icy slab.

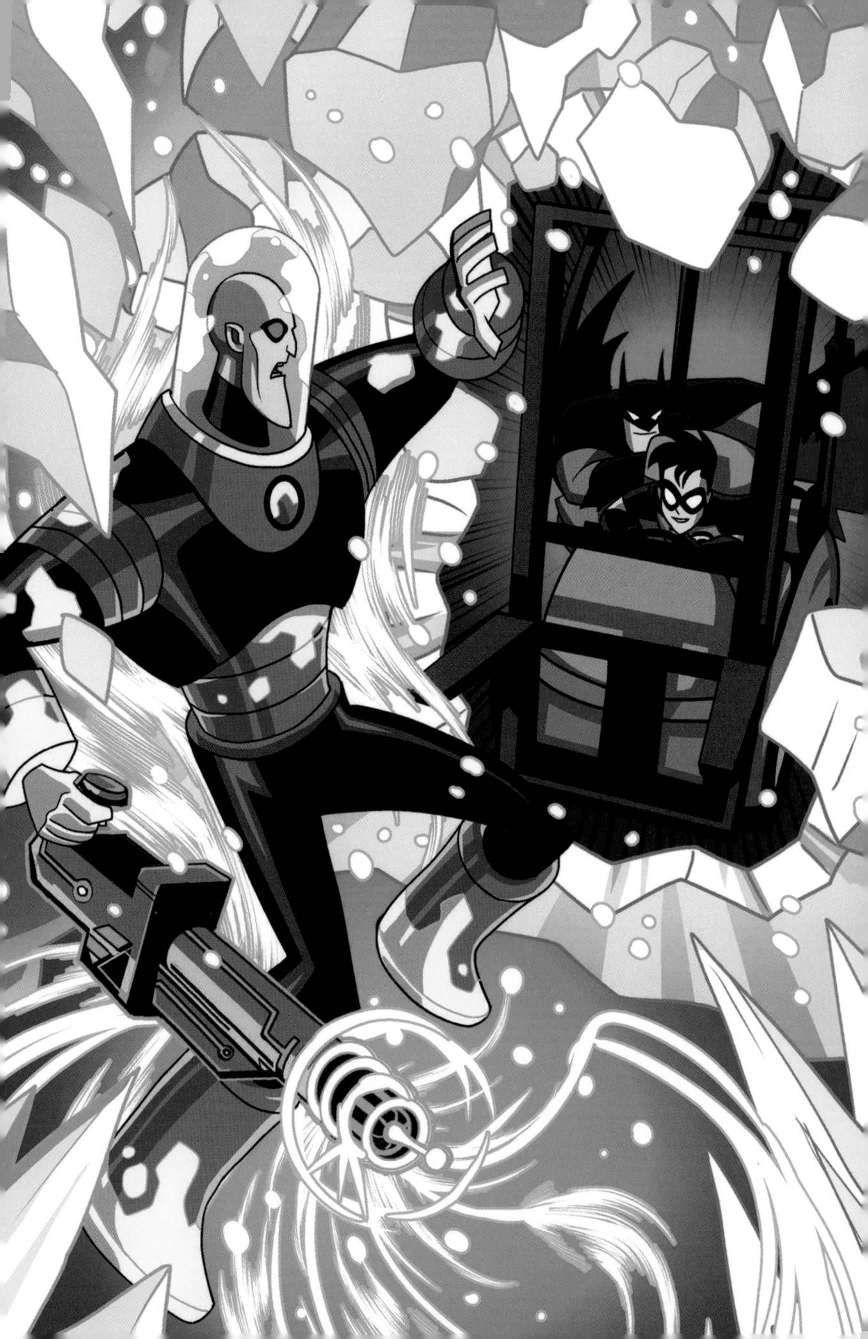

Batman and Robin start to warm up.

"Your Zone of Cold is slipping away," says the Boy Wonder.

The dazed Mr. Freeze snatches at the necklace in Batman's hand. The Dark Knight tosses the treasure to Robin.

"Out of reach and out of luck," Batman says. "You should have known we'd be waiting for you."

"Know what else is waiting?" Robin says with a smile. "The Gotham City police and a nice warm cell!"

"What should we do with this freeze ray, Robin?"

"It will make a *cool* trophy in the Batcave, Batman."

"Good idea. You deserve this trophy."

"I do?"

"Yes, for getting Mr. Freeze to *fork* it over!"

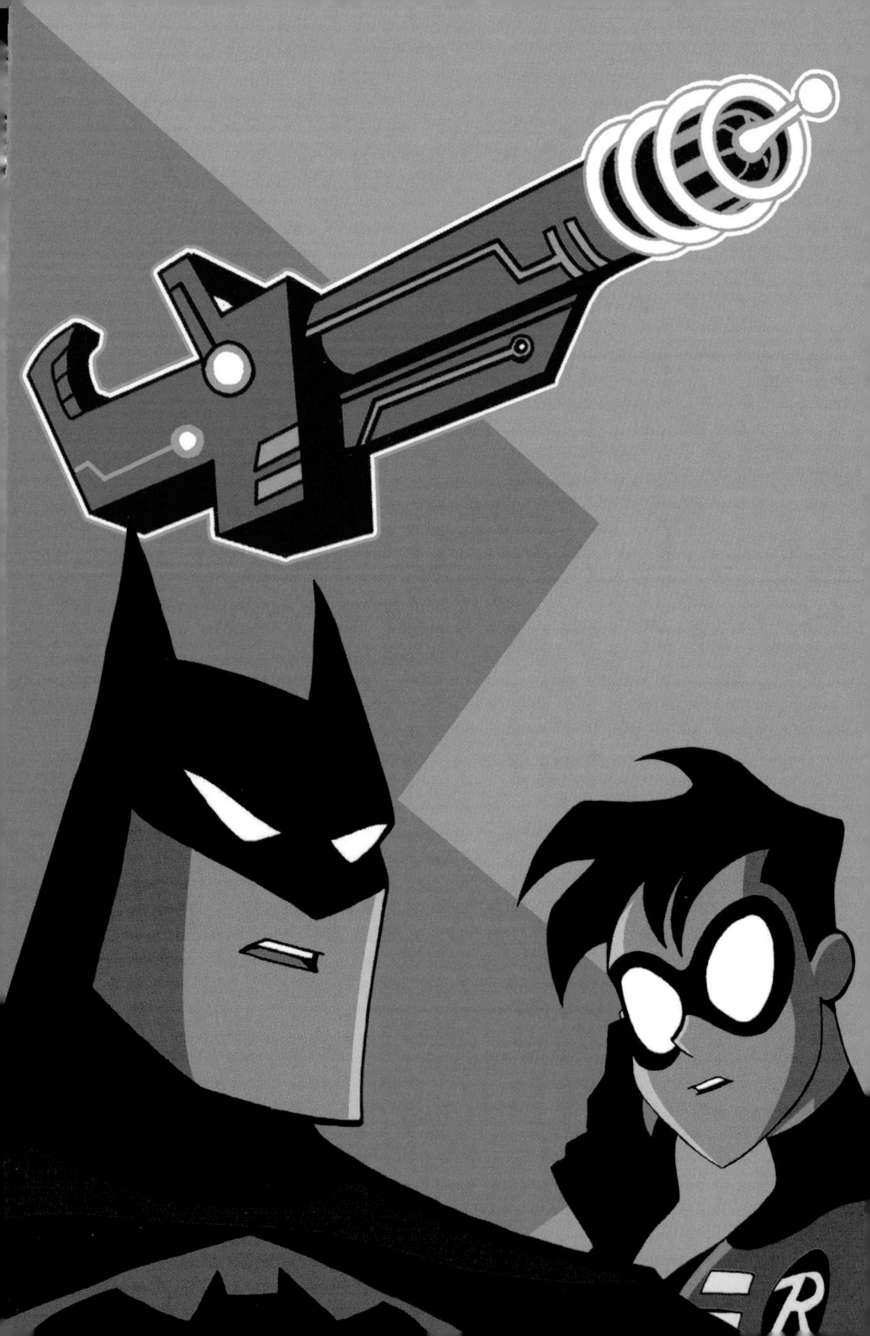

GLOSSARY

cargo (KAHR-goh)—the goods carried by a ship, vehicle, or aircraft

chute (SHOOT)—a narrow slide

disguise (dis-GYZ)—a costume that helps someone hide what they really look like

forklift (FORK-lift)—a vehicle with two prongs in the front that is used to lift and carry loads

frost (FRAWST)—a very thin layer of ice

gag (GAG)—something put over the mouth to stop someone from making noise

maximum (MAK-suh-muhm)—the greatest possible amount, or the upper limit

patrol (puh-TROHL)—to walk or travel around an area to protect it or to keep watch

warehouse (WAIR-hous)—a large building used for storing or sending goods such as packages and letters

zone (ZOHN)—an area that is separate from other areas

DISCUSS

1. Have you ever felt so cold you could hardly move or talk? Describe what it felt like.

2. Why does Mr. Freeze wear a glass helmet? Do you think that it's for protection or for something else?

3. When Mr. Freeze flees the jewelry store, Batman stays behind to rescue Robin. Do you have good friends that you would help if they were in trouble?

WRITE

1. Mr. Freeze uses his freeze ray to make a giant ice slide. If you had a machine like that, what would you make? Describe it and write a paragraph about what you would do with it.

2. Robin is disguised at the end of the story in order to fool Mr. Freeze. Write a short story where Batman uses a disguise to catch a different crook.

3. The Zone of Cold causes anyone inside it to feel intense cold. Could there be other kinds of zone machines? Would the Joker have a Zone of Laughs? Would Catwoman have a Zone of Purrs? Write a list of other kinds of zones that could be used by heroes or by villains. Describe how they work.

Author

Michael Dahl is the prolific author of the best-selling *Goodnight Baseball* picture book and more than 200 other books for children and young adults. He has won the AEP Distinguished Achievement Award three times for his nonfiction, a Teachers' Choice Award from *Learning* magazine, and a Seal of Excellence from the Creative Child Awards. He is also the author of the Hocus Pocus Hotel mystery series and the Dragonblood books. Dahl currently lives in Minneapolis, Minnesota.

Illustrator

Luciano Vecchio was born in 1982 and is based in Buenos Aires, Argentina. A freelance artist for many projects at Marvel and DC Comics, his work has been seen in print and online around the world. He has illustrated many DC Super Heroes books for Capstone, and some of his recent comic work includes *Beware the Batman*, *Green Lantern: The Animated Series*, *Young Justice*, *Ultimate Spider-Man*, and his creator owned web-comic, *Sereno*.